THE NIGHT BEFORE

THE NIGHT BEFORE

A SHORT STORY

JACK DANE

ALSO BY JACK DANE

Only one thing is for certain...it's not going to be a silent night.

Struggling private chef Holly is elated to finally score her first big gig–preparing a Christmas Eve dinner for a **wealthy family** in a massive mansion.

It's the opportunity of a lifetime, the kind that could finally get her business off the ground. Given what's happened in her life recently, she really needs the win.

But when Holly arrives, ready to cook for at least a dozen, she finds the house **empty**. Not a creature is stirring, not even a mouse. The lights are on, the place is decorated floor-to-ceiling, but there is not **one. Single. Person**.

Something is very, **very** wrong.

Then comes a knock at the door—and it isn't Santa Claus.

As the sky darkens and snow falls, one fact becomes **terrifyingly** clear...it's not going to be a silent night.

ONE

I set down my phone with a groan and rub my forehead.

Another killer call with Mom. Bless her for checking in of course, but it certainly doesn't feel good knowing I have to frequently share just how well my business isn't doing.

She offered to loan me some money to cover rent this month. Again.

I turned her down last month, but this time around I had no choice but to accept, as much as I didn't want to. It's the last week of December, which means January rent will be due all too soon.

And with Nick having moved out, I'm the only one on the hook this time around.

Though she was sympathetic, I could tell what Mom was really thinking.

Holly, what a huge mistake you've made starting a private chef business.

And honestly, maybe she's right. I run a hand through

my hair to detangle it as I glance toward my apartment window.

The world outside is drab and gray. It mirrors how I feel, despite the countdown to Christmas.

Nothing will kill holiday cheer like a good breakup and coming to terms with the fact that you might have to give up on your dreams, too.

Even as the thought crosses my mind, I instinctively fight back.

I can't go back to working a lifeless, soul-sucking corporate job. I just can't. I honestly think If I have to spend another hour seated on a stiff chair in a blank white cubicle spewing corporate jargon, I'll go crazy.

Letting out a sigh, I push out of my desk chair and move up to the window.

It just *looks* cold out there. I can tell that without having to step outside. The radiator whistles against my sweatpants, sending blasts of heat up my body that make goosebumps rise across my skin.

Down on the street, a few brave passersby trudge through the dirty slush that has accumulated on the side-walks from the last snowfall. It didn't remain pure and white for long, that's for sure.

Nothing does in this city.

Certainly not my dream of being a private chef. What started out as a brilliant, passionate idea is now more akin to that streaky sludge out on the sidewalk– beaten down and trod all over.

Maybe Mom and Nicholas are right. Maybe it's time I stop chasing my dream and just fall in line again like everyone else has.

Who am I, really, to think that I could start my own private chef company?

I'm just a girl who loves to cook. Yes, I love it more than everything else in the world, but maybe that's not enough.

My breath fogs up the windowpane as I look out at the buildings around me. The little cloud obscures the view. Supposedly we're going to get a decent amount of snow tomorrow, making for a white Christmas and Christmas Eve, too.

Even that isn't enough to brighten my mood. Pressing a finger up to the window-cloud, I draw a little frowny face and then step away.

Out in the kitchen area, I hear Kris pull a pan out from the cabinet.

"Holly, get your sad butt in here–we're making Christmas cookies," she hollers, her voice echoing through the apartment.

I step over to my door and open it enough to jam my head through.

"I'm not sad, K."

Kris straightens up from bending over a cabinet to give me a look, her eyebrow raised.

"Are we still pretending the walls in this place aren't as thin as toilet paper? I might as well have been on that call to your Mom with you, babes."

She heaves a bag of cookie dough onto the countertop with a grunt before speaking again.

"I know it's been a tough month for you—so we're making cookies, understood? Time to make Holly *jolly* again," she says.

I roll my eyes at the pun but smile inwardly as my heart fills. Kris is my best friend in the city, and I don't know what I'd do without her.

"And turn on the Christmas tree lights, would you? Looks like it's starting to get dark," Kris says over her shoulder.

I cross through the kitchen and into our tiny living room, which is little more than a loveseat placed across from a TV stand.

That didn't stop Kris from buying a nearly six-foot tall Christmas tree, though. We've got it wedged right up into the corner, which is about the only place it can reasonably fit in here–as long as you ignore the errant branches that slightly obscure the TV screen.

Stepping on the button, I watch the strands of lights wrapped around our tree come to life. It adds a wonderful warmth to the apartment that makes me feel better almost instantly.

There's just a coziness to Christmas lights, especially the soft yellow ones we used to decorate this tree.

Reminds me of being a kid again. Back when my biggest worry was trying to figure out what Santa had wrapped up for me and placed under the tree.

Nowadays, life is a little more complicated.

"Give me a hand, would you?"

Kris's voice snaps me out of my thoughts, and I rejoin her in the kitchen. Together we roll balls of dough into a flat sheet and then use cookie cutter shapes to cut out cookies shaped like gingerbread men, Christmas trees, and ornaments.

It's sticky, messy, and absolutely what I needed to get my mind off of everything else right now.

By the time the cookies are baked and painted with icing, I'm feeling a whole lot better. I don't want to say it's the magic of the season–I'm not that cheesy–but somehow, someway, maybe things will turn out okay.

After the kitchen has been cleaned, Kris and I crash on the couch. She reaches for the remote to see if there's anything to watch, while I pull out my phone.

There's a text from Mom waiting for me, saying how much she loves me. I've got a few email notifications, too.

As I tap on those to see what was sent, my heart skips a beat.

My gasp snaps Kris's head over to me.

"What–did Meg finally break up with Aaron?"

"What..." I start and then shake my head.

"No–someone responded to my post about the private chef business," I say, the words tumbling out of me.

My hands feel shaky as Kris lets out an excited scream.

"Oh my–Holly, this is huge! What'd they say? Read it to me."

The pounding of my heart inside my chest is making it a little hard to focus on the tiny words on my phone screen, but I do my best.

"Hello Chef Holly, my name is Barbara Garland. I apologize for the late notice, and I really hope you'll be available at this late date, but I am desperate. The chef we booked to prepare the annual Garland Family Christmas Eve Dinner at our estate has had to cancel because of a family emergency," I say, my voice picking up in pitch and volume with each sequential word.

"I found your listing and am hoping you might be interested in the job. I know you'd probably rather set your own menu, but all the necessary groceries have already been delivered to the house, and maybe with so little notice, that's a good thing? All that would be required on your part is your talent in the kitchen. I can send along the menu if you need to see it before making your decision. I would of course be happy to pay for your transportation and offer a nice bonus as well because of the horribly late notice."

Now both of us are screaming and jumping up and down. I'm so happy I could cry. In fact, I am crying—hot tears of joy and relief stream down my cheeks as Kris and I hug.

This is it—my first customer. The fact it's tomorrow on Christmas Eve is only a minor inconvenience.

I'm an only child, which meant Christmas dinners were always just us three. Now with Dad gone, and Mom traveling full-time in her retirement, I was planning to tag along with Kris to spend the holidays with her family.

"Oh no," she says, realizing what this means. "You won't be able to come home with me tomorrow to spend Christmas with my family."

"I know. But maybe I could take the train there myself on Christmas Day? I have to do this, Kris. I need the money, and... it's my dream."

"You bet it is," she says with a big smile on her face. "This is going to lead to all kinds of good things, I know it."

"It is. I think it's exactly the jumpstart I need," I say.

Sounds like this "family dinner" involves a pretty prestigious family, too, if they have an estate.

If this goes well, this could change absolutely everything for me. It all starts with one, and this just might be mine.

Maybe Christmas miracles really do happen.

TWO

I awaken the next morning to find white snowflakes coming down outside my window.

It's a total flurry of them, blanketing the grey city with a fresh new coat of white. I can't help but smile as I watch the flakes come down.

A white Christmas. Given the news of last night, this just feels even more magical.

I've got to catch a train upstate though, so hopefully this doesn't interfere with transportation too much. The Garland family estate is up in the Hudson Valley, according to Barbara's email.

It also mentioned I'd be preparing a meal for upwards of fifteen people. Talk about trial by fire.

Maybe I should feel nervous, but honestly, I don't. I'm ready for it—ready to prove how much I want this.

So fifteen rich people in a palatial home upstate? Bring it on.

This is my chance, and I'm not going to blow it.

Even though the Christmas Eve Dinner won't be

until tonight, I'll need to get there several hours in advance to prepare everything. That means my butt needs to be in a train seat within the hour, given the travel time to get up to the Hudson Valley.

Kris's door cracks open as I gulp down a cup of coffee in the kitchen.

"Headed out?" she asks, her eyes barely open.

I nod. She shuffles over to me, still in her pajamas, and gives me a hug.

"So proud of you," she says, her voice muffled against my shoulder.

"When are you heading home?" I ask as we separate.

Kris shrugs. "I don't know. I'll definitely be going back to bed first, that's for sure."

She's from New Jersey, which means she can take the commuter train to her family's home. The ride is only an hour or so.

I pull her into another hug, squeezing her tight.

"Tell everyone I said hey, okay?" I say.

She nods. "Will do. Now go be the best Christmas chef ever."

Stepping outside of the apartment makes me gasp a little as the cold air hits my face. Snowflakes continue to flutter down around me, blanketing everything in sight. There appears to be almost an inch on the ground already, with more to come. Much more.

Kris said there was a chance it could be the biggest snowstorm in years.

That makes my stomach tighten a little, as the possibility of too *much* snow ruining my big chef debut crosses my mind.

As I hike down the crowded sidewalk and adjust my beanie, I send up a little prayer that nothing like that goes wrong. When I get to Grand Central Station and have functional use of my hands again, I'll check my weather app for the updated snowfall estimates.

Until then, it's a matter of fast-walking through the crowds, sometimes stepping down into the street slush to continue at my preferred pace. The price of the train ticket was absolutely exorbitant, given that I'm literally leaving on Christmas Eve and I only bought it last night.

Thankfully, Barbara sent me money for the ticket alongside the email about the menu. Too much money, in fact. Clearly, these are people to whom money is not really an issue.

That means I'll have to really impress them with my cooking. No doubt these are some refined palettes I'll be dealing with.

Still, I know I can do it. This is what I want, after all.

As I funnel into the crowded subway with everyone else, I do so with a little smile on my face. Getting paid to make good food. A dream come true.

My stomach is fluttery the whole ride, even when the subway car screeches to a halt in the middle of the dark tunnel. Seconds pass, and then we start moving again.

I make it to Grand Central about fifteen minutes before my train is set to depart.

Every time I come here, I can't help but be amazed at the sheer size of the place. All the movies featuring it don't do it justice. It really does have to be experienced.

Especially at Christmastime with the Christmas market and all the decorations. Giant wreaths hang on every wall, glistening golden and red ornaments adorning them.

Combined with the happy crowds and strings of Christmas lights, it's like something straight out of a post-card. I pause for a moment in the main hall, just allowing the buzz of commotion to wash over me. Everyone is hustling to get home for the big day.

I need to be moving quickly too, if I want to get a decent seat on my train. After a quick peek at the board to see which track I'm on, I head in that direction, moving fast like the holiday travelers around me.

There's a noticeable buzz of excitement in the air, a general sense of energy that fills me as I get to the train. Aboard it, the other passengers talk and laugh as we all get settled.

Once I get into my seat, I pull out my phone and check the weather. One hundred percent chance of snowfall—that's fairly obvious.

Wow. Looks like there's a chance we could get almost a foot of snow today with more expected tomorrow. That's definitely a lot in such a short time span.

Then again, I'm going to the Hudson Valley. They're no strangers to heavy snowfall in upstate New York. People there probably know how to handle it.

Stuffing my phone back into my pocket, I focus on getting into a comfortable position.

Soon enough, we're pulling out of Grand Central and headed upstate. It's a good few minutes before the view outside my window is anything but buildings, but soon enough I get to look out at the winter wonderland that upstate New York has become.

Draped in snow like this, everything just feels a little bit more wonderful. I cozy up against the window and watch the snow-covered scenery as the train speeds down the track.

Before long, I'll be at the Garland estate and elbow-deep in cooking prep. My chest flutters again.

There's no doubt about it... after today, my life will be forever changed.

THREE

It's snowing pretty heavily by the time the train pulls into the Hudson station.

Enough so that I'm starting to get a little nervous.

The parking lot beyond the track is covered in a thick layer of white that's only getting thicker. If this keeps up, we might really have a record-breaking storm.

I won't let it stop me, though. Rain or shine—or snow, I should say—I'm getting this job done.

There are a few other people who've deboarded the train with me, their coats pulled tight around them as they drag suitcases through the snowy blanket on the train platform.

I've only got a backpack, as once the meal is finished, I'll take the train back. That is, unless the snow doesn't let up and the trains can't run.

My shoes push through the fluffy white stuff as I make my way down the platform steps with careful precision. All across the parking lot, people are scraping the snow off their dashboards.

Since I don't have a car, I pull out my phone with a shivering hand and call a rideshare through an app.

It says my driver will be here in five minutes. I head for the small brick ticket office building next to the parking lot, as I don't think I'm tough enough to spend all five minutes out here waiting.

The bottom of my shoes squeak as I step inside. The floor is wet and slick from everyone's tracked sludge. All but one of the ticket counters are shuttered, and I don't see anyone in the available booth.

Rows of bench seats are splayed out in front of me, so I head over and plop down.

Now that I'm indoors, the heat trapped inside all my layers is overwhelming. I'm getting hot flashes as I hurriedly unzip myself. A quick look at my phone tells me the driver is still five minutes out.

Probably just the weather, forcing him to drive slowly. I don't blame him—I certainly wouldn't want to be behind the wheel in this, and a cautious driver is a good thing, right?

After what feels like forever, I get a notification from my phone telling me the driver is outside. With a quick zip of my coat, I trudge back out into the flurry.

It's still early afternoon right now, so a weak winter sun illuminates the world around me. In just a few short hours, it'll be pitch black.

I'm glad it isn't yet, because I can already hardly see with the heaviness of the snowfall. The red glow of tail-lights against a snowbank directs my eyes to the waiting car.

It's a black sedan. Not exactly built for this kind of

weather, but it'll have to do. Making my way toward it, I look around the parking lot once more.

Someone else is standing outside the ticket office, waiting, but they shuffle inside as I turn. Probably thought this was their car.

I grab hold of the door handle with a mittened-hand and slide inside, welcoming the blast of heat that hits my face as I do.

After exchanging a greeting with the driver, we're pulling out of the parking lot and back out onto the street. It appears to have been recently plowed, which is good.

Still, the snow is coming down fast and hard enough that it's already begun to blanket over the dark asphalt again, making it look like it's been sprinkled with sugar.

I look out the back seat window at the town around us as we drive. Barbara's email said the Garland house is a bit outside the main area of town, meaning it'll be another half hour or so until I reach it.

The view of houses outside my window soon turns to thickly wooded forests.

Definitely pays to be wealthy, that's for sure. I'm already envious of the Garland estate, and I haven't even seen it yet. Probably because I'm starting to get a little sick of my teensy apartment.

Out here, there's just so much space. I settle into the seat as the snow-laden trees whip by.

When I'm a successful millionaire chef, I think I'd like to get a little place out here. Maybe a cute weekend cabin I can retreat to when the city gets too hectic. That thought puts a small smile on my face.

Finally, we turn onto the road where the Garland

estate is located. I haven't seen another house for at least ten minutes.

The car finally rolls to a stop outside a gated entrance. Flanking either side are large square pillars made of cobblestone, which connect to a stone wall that runs off into the distance in both directions.

The gate is already open for us, and previous tire tracks through the snow provide a clear path down the winding driveway as the driver turns into it. If it weren't for those, I'm not sure this little car would've been able to do it.

The ride is bumpier now as we head up toward the house which is starting to come into view through the thick trees. And then I realize calling it a *house* is really not the right term.

The enormous mansion that presents itself to us as we clear the treeline and enter the circular driveway looks like something straight out of *Clue*, complete with Victorian spikes running along the roof.

Towers rise up overhead, windows reflecting the glow of the snow back to me.

Definitely gorgeous. A little ominous, too.

Oh well. I don't have to live here, I just need to cook. I can't wait to see the kitchen. I'm betting it's state of the art.

After I step out of the car, the driver pulls around the rest of the circle and starts back down the bumpy driveway. No doubt he wants to get home to his own Christmas Eve celebration.

I turn back to the Garland mansion.

There's a large stone front porch area with a balcony

overhead, but Barbara told me to enter through the servant's entrance on the right side.

Rich people stuff, whatever. So, trudging through the drifts of snow, I make my way around the length of the house and turn the corner.

There's the entrance up ahead. I think if there weren't inches of snow on the ground, I'd probably see a gravel driveway leading up to the side door for delivery vans.

This entrance is much less grand than the front, with only a simple pair of black doors.

As I walk toward it, the windows to my left reveal snippets of the home's interior. It appears to be heavily decorated for the season.

Strings of Christmas lights line the interior of the glass, wrapped around garlands with pine cones and red berries.

Now that I'm closer to the house, I can also just make out the muffled sound of vintage Christmas music echoing from somewhere inside. Sounds like "Rockin' Around the Christmas Tree" by Brenda Lee.

The snow is still light and fluffy underfoot, which would make it fairly easy to trek through—if I weren't wearing the clogs I always cook in.

As I come up to the double doors, my teeth let out a chatter. Sure is chilly out here. I can't wait to get inside and get the oven started, that'll really warm me up.

I come to a stop in front of the doors, my heartbeat picking up just a little. This is it.

Pulling off my hat, I hurriedly run a hand through my hair to try and smooth it all down. Under my coat I'm wearing the black chef's coat Mom gave me last Christmas.

Hopefully it makes me seem more professional.

Raising a numb hand, I rap against the hard surface of the door.

FOUR

I wait almost a minute before deciding to knock again.

This time, my hand comes down with more force, the knock echoing loudly against my ears in the silent snowfall around me. I wince a little. The door feeling like it's made of stone against my cold, bare knuckles.

Even after the second try, there's still no response from inside that would make me think someone heard me. No one opens the door, and I can't hear anything apart from the Christmas music. In fact the song is actually a little clearer now that I'm standing so close.

Can the staff not hear me knocking because of the music?

My teeth chatter again as I debate what to do. Leaning my head forward, I try to put my ear up to the door without touching it to try and see if I can pick up any sounds of commotion from inside.

It doesn't sound like anyone is in the kitchen at all. *Fantastic.* My first real gig, and it's already off to quite the awkward start.

I don't want to trudge back around to the front of the house again and ring the doorbell, because Barbara explicitly stated I should use the service entrance. The last thing I need to do is piss off my one and only customer by disobeying her instructions.

Letting out a breath that steams the cold air in front of me, I raise my hand to knock again but then lower it.

The door handle is right there. I wonder if... maybe they just left it unlocked for me?

Gripping the handle, I find that the door is indeed unlocked. It swings wide open, emitting a blast of warm air and revealing an expansive kitchen.

"Hello?" I call out. "It's me, Holly... the chef?"

After a moment, I step inside. That must've been what Barbara meant by "use the service entrance." She must have intended for me to let myself in.

Stepping inside, I let out a shiver and shake off a few of the snowflakes that had landed on my head, wiping my Birkenstock clogs—also a gift from my mom—so I don't track water inside the house. Then I look around the kitchen.

Directly in front of me is the largest kitchen island I've ever seen, more like something you'd find in an industrial kitchen than a private home.

Above it, pots and pans of all shapes and sizes hang down from racks suspended from the ceiling. Surrounding me on all four walls is more counter space, complete with cabinets above and drawers underneath.

There's the stove over there, a Viking Tuscany series with six burners.

Kitchen knives hang from another rack, with even

more utensils dangling beside them. A stack of thick wooden cutting boards rests up against the tiled backsplash. This place is fully supplied.

What I don't see, however, are any people.

It's just me in this enormous kitchen, and that's slightly off-putting. Stepping off the absorbant doormat, I take a couple steps toward the door that I assume leads into the rest of the house.

"Hello?" I call out again. "It's Holly, from Cheftastic. I'm here."

While I'm pretty sure Barbara left the side door unlocked so I could enter, I just want to be super sure I'm not catching anyone by surprise here.

No one responds, and there are no sounds save for the music, which is now Elvis's "Blue Christmas". Now that I'm inside, the volume is much louder, and it's quickly becoming clear why no one heard me knocking.

They've *really* got Elvis cranked up.

I take a few more steps into the home, my shoes squeaking on the checkerboard tile floor.

"Hello, Cheftastic here," I call again.

A bead of sweat rolls down my temple as I wait for anyone to respond. It's really warm in here.

Unzipping my jacket, I come up to the kitchen entryway. The door is a pocket door, which slides neatly into the wall as I gently pull it open. Once it's tucked away, I put a hand on each side of the frame and poke my head through.

I'm looking out at one of the largest dining rooms I've ever stepped foot in. It's got to be at least thirty feet long, with ceilings so high it makes the room feel more like a castle hall than a place to eat food.

Taking up most of the space in the center of the room is the massive dark brown dining table, no doubt hand-crafted from some very expensive wood. A fancy white tablecloth has been draped over the table's surface in preparation for tonight's meal.

It's already set with the plates and cutlery, all a glittering gold. Red candles of varying heights extend down the length of the table, with more lit garland wrapping around the bases. They are lit already, though dinner is a few hours away.

The floorboards creak underneath me as I step fully into the room. The music drifting through the house is now "White Christmas" by Bing Crosby.

Hunter green walls seem to absorb most of the candlelight as I move through the space, giving it a rather haunting feel as I keep calling out to let the homeowners know I'm here.

Maybe they're upstairs and can't hear anything on the first floor. A house like this one would have pretty superior insulation, I'm sure.

"Hello?" I shout.

Walking to the other side of the room, I reach another doorway. This one is double-door width, and leads out into the main room.

There's the front door across the way, the windows whited out from the flurry as I scan the living room and foyer for any signs of life.

A massive stone fireplace sits off to my left, the hearth

roaring with flame that crackles and pops. That explains the toasty temperature in here.

That fireplace is so large I could probably lie down flat inside it. Santa won't have any trouble getting down *this* chimney.

Garland snakes across the mantle, with Christmas cards in front. My eyes move over them, settling on one that says *Merry Christmas from the DeLucas!* before moving on.

In the corner nearest to me is a Christmas tree that has to be at least fifteen feet tall. It's wrapped in sprawling chains of warm golden Christmas lights, big red ornaments, and bows.

Whoever decorated this place clearly spared no expense.

Lining the base of the tree are gift boxes, their shiny wrapping paper reflecting the glow from the fireplace.

My feet come to a stop at the edge of the ornate rug that sprawls out before me. Plenty of festive decor, but still no people.

This is starting to get a little weird.

"Hello?" I call out.

My eyes travel to a pair of bookcases up against the base of the staircase to my right. On one of the shelves is a large tablet, its glowing screen displaying the current song choice. The source of the blasting music.

After a moment of deliberation, I walk over to it. There's a large pause button right there on the screen.

Should I press it? I go back and forth in my mind but decide to do it. I'm done playing hide and seek. In fact, I've really got to get moving on the food prep.

My finger comes down against the screen, and the music turns off instantly.

The deafening silence is jarring.

"Hello? It's Holly. I'm here to prepare dinner," I shout again, really straining my voice this time.

I wait a second for someone to reply.

But there's nothing. Nothing but the crackle of the fireplace behind me and the gentle whoosh of the snow outside.

Okay, this is officially very strange.

Everything around me is perfectly done up—the decorations, the table, the warm hearth—and yet there's not a single soul in sight.

It's like everyone just… disappeared.

Suddenly the atmosphere around me doesn't feel quite so charming.

Christmas time evokes feelings of togetherness, of spending time together. With a lack of anyone to spend time with, the whole display is quite jarring.

My heart thuds against my ribcage as I stand there, mind racing. Where is everyone? What am I supposed to do here?

It seems like the whole Garland family left to do their Christmas shopping and left me entirely alone in their massive mansion.

Do they really want me to—

The shrill echo of a doorbell through the halls cuts my thoughts short.

Someone's here.

FIVE

I move quickly toward the door as my pulse thuds in my ears.

Maybe it's one of the family members. But if it was, wouldn't they just enter?

I don't know what's going on. Hopefully whoever is out there can give me some explanation.

The doors are several feet taller than I am and made from a wood similar in color to the dining table. Grabbing hold of one of the handles, I tug it open.

It's heavier than expected, but any thoughts of strain go out the window when I see who's standing outside.

"Carol?" I ask, utterly confused.

Carol's head snaps around, her eyes widening. Out of anyone I might have expected to find on the doorstep, I think my ex-boyfriend's ex-girlfriend was last on the list.

She looks just as surprised to see me as I am to see her.

"Holly? What are you doing here?" she asks me.

I blink. She's saying it like she's the one who's supposed to be here, not me.

"I'm preparing the Christmas Eve dinner," I start.

Carol's brow furrows. "What? But I thought you guys broke up."

I'm so lost right now. She's talking about Nick, but what does he have to do with this? Carol seems to sense my bewilderment, and her eyes widen again.

"Don't you know? This is like... Nick's family home. Where he grew up," she says.

I feel like I've been slapped. My entire face tingles as my mind reels, trying to piece all this together.

This is *Nick's* home?

Then who are the Garlands?

"But... some woman named Barbara Garland told me to come here, to prepare the meal for tonight," I say, stuttering over my words as I try to get my brain functioning again.

Carol shakes her head, still looking at me.

"I have no idea who that is. How could you not know this is Nick's house?"

My head shakes now. "I... we only dated for like six months. And he never told me he came from—" I wave my hand around, "—all this."

Carol chews her lip. "Well now I'm really confused, because Nick told me to meet him here, that we needed to talk. I figured it was because you guys had broken up... but why would he invite you too?"

"He didn't," I say. "I told you, I got an email from some *Garland* woman asking me to come and cook the dinner. If I had known this was Nick's place, I never would've showed up."

A gust of wind blows a wall of snow at both of us, the flecks stinging my face as I stand in the doorway.

Carol lets out a shiver and steps past me to come inside. I remain in the doorway for another moment, staring out at the white world around us in search of answers.

Nothing out there but more snow. Finally, I pull myself back inside and shut the door.

Carol is already taking her gloves off as she looks around the entry hall.

"Did *you* do all this?" Carol asks with a gesture to the decorations. "Nick said his family is at their chalet in Gstaad for the winter."

I shake my head, too shocked to speak. There's just so much weird stuff going on right now I don't even know where to start.

Carol shrugs. "Hmm. Guess Nick did it then. Didn't realize he was such a Christmas guy. Where is he? Is—"

My hands come up. I've heard enough.

"Carol—there's no one here. At least not that I've seen. No Nick, no one. I showed up because I thought this was my big break, but now I don't know *what* is going on."

I feel a little light-headed and lean against the staircase bannister for support. It finally seems to dawn on Carol that something very strange is going on here.

"So... both of us got invited here," she starts, and I nod.

"But there's no one home," Carol finishes.

"No. I mean, I haven't searched the whole house, but I haven't seen anyone. It's actually really creepy."

Just as I finish speaking, a creak sounds overhead. Both of our eyes flick upward as my blood runs cold.

"You don't think..." Carol says in a low voice.

Then she straightens up.

"Nick? Is that you?" she shouts.

Her voice is so loud it makes me wince. We both wait but there's no reply. Carol swallows hard, her eyes flicking back to me.

"He's got to be here. He's just... hiding for whatever stupid reason. You know how actors are—everything is always so theatrical."

I want to agree with her, but why would Nick do this?

I broke up with him a couple weeks ago, and we've had zero contact since.

If he wanted to get back together with me, why the smoke and mirrors?

And why have Carol show up, too?

My stomach twists. I don't like this.

Carol still seems to think this is all some sort of weird prank, but I'm not so sure. The whole thing just feels... off.

Carol's still looking up the staircase, as if she expects Nick to pop out at any second and yell, "Surprise!" And maybe he will.

He'll have a lot of explaining to do, but at least we'd have an answer.

After another second, she puts her foot on the first step.

"What are you doing?" I ask.

"What? You said you didn't search the whole house, right? I'm gonna find Nick and beat an apology out of him for whatever stupid waste of time this is," Carol replies. "It cost me a small fortune for the stupid ride-share, and the guy wouldn't even come up the driveway because it wasn't plowed. I had to hoof it up here through the snow in *these*."

She points down to indicate her expensive-looking high-heeled shoes, which appear to be ruined.

I swallow. "Why don't we just... why don't we just call him?"

Carol thinks for a moment and then shrugs. "Okay, yeah."

She pulls out her phone and finds Nick in her contacts before pressing the call button.

Placing the phone on speaker mode, she holds it up between us. My ears are primed to hear the ring of a phone from somewhere upstairs, but it's silent.

In fact, the call never goes through. A *no-service* message flashes across the screen, and the call drops.

Carol rolls her eyes. "Ugh."

"Probably the storm," I say.

"No, it's always spotty out here," she says. "You saw how much land they have."

Pocketing her phone again, she wipes her palms on her thighs and glances back upstairs.

"There had better be a *really* good explanation for this. To think I cancelled plans to be here," she says, starting up the stairs.

I chew my lip. I'm not sure what it is about this house,

but it's really starting to give me the creeps. I hustle up the steps after her.

"So Nick told you to meet him here?" I ask.

Carol nods. "Yeah. Out of the blue, he texts me and says I need to meet him at his family's house, that he had something super important to tell me."

Clearly, Nick wanted both of us here.

He came up with some fake identity and job offer to get me to show up, because he knew I wouldn't otherwise.

The only question now is—why?

SIX

The light outside has just begun to fade as we conclude our search of the upstairs rooms.

The final room we searched is a massive bedroom, sporting a king-sized mattress with curtained bedposts like Ebeneezer Scrooge's bed in *A Christmas Carol*.

Carol's shoulders lower as she stares down at the empty bed, her arm holding the curtains apart. That makes it official.

We are alone in the house.

"Okay," Carol says, her voice shaking slightly, "this is weird."

I nod silently. With each consecutive room that we've searched, the knot in my stomach has grown tighter and tighter.

This is looking less and less like a prank and more like something much more sinister.

I just want to know what's going on.

Why did Nick get me out here, to the middle of nowhere in upstate New York?

I was so excited and eager to close my first client that I didn't do any sort of research into where I was really going. There didn't seem to be any need to.

Now here I am, in a massive remote mansion with no cell service and a snowstorm that's only getting worse.

Carol comes back over to me, running a hand through her hair. She stops at one of the bedroom windows and peers out.

"It's really coming down out there," she says. "Like, it's almost a blizzard."

Because it's the dead of winter, the sun sets in the mid-afternoon. Before too much longer, it's going to be pitch-black outside.

"Should we try and hike out of here?" Carol asks.

I look down at her high-heels and my slip-on chef's shoes and weigh the possibility.

Neither of us is dressed for being outside in the freezing cold for very long. Especially not in conditions like this, with the snow coming down as hard as it is.

Within the hour, it's going to be dark.

If we got lost out there, which is a distinct possibility, we'd be in big trouble.

"How far away are the neighbors?" I ask.

Carol thinks it over and then sighs. "Too far. There really aren't any."

Visibility is near zero right now. As much as I don't like it, it looks like we'll be here for the foreseeable future, at least until the storm ends.

"I think we're stuck here tonight," I say.

"So what, we're just supposed to wait around here all day? It's Christmas Eve," Carol says, "You saw how much snow is coming down out there. They might not get the roads cleared for *days*."

That sends a chill down my spine. Trapped here for potentially days with no way to call for help.

"I just don't get it," Carol says, stepping away from the window as she throws her hands up. "Why bring us here?"

"And why both of us?" I ask as I continue to stare outside.

The sky is darkening quickly. As unnerving as all of this is now, it's bound to get a whole lot worse once the sun goes down.

"Is it some form of punishment? Some dumb way of getting back at us?" Carol asks.

I think back to what I know about Nick. One of the main reasons I broke up with him was his emotional outbursts.

He liked to say he was passionate, that it was just part of being an actor. Bottling up his feelings would stifle his performances, he'd say.

A little less romantic of an idea when you're sitting there at dinner watching him berate the waiter who forgot to add sliced avocado to his burger.

So yeah, I suppose this could be some weird form of punishment for us. Maybe he's still mad at me for breaking up with him. It certainly did seem to catch him by surprise, though it was hardly a surprise to anyone around me.

Whatever the reason is, we're here now. Most likely for the whole night in fact.

"There'd better be food here somewhere," Carol says. "Otherwise this whole–"

Her words cut off instantly as the first few notes of "Last Christmas" by Wham! suddenly fill the air.

The music has been turned back on.

SEVEN

Carol's wide eyes meet mine.

Neither of us speak, our breath caught in our throats as we strain our ears. But with the music blasting again, it's impossible to make out much of anything.

"Nick?" Carol asks me.

I don't respond. I don't know if I want it to be him or not, at this point.

The song continues to play, and the world doesn't erupt into chaos. After thirty seconds, my heart rate has started to go down just a little.

Moving for the door brings Carol's hand snapping up to grip my arm. I look back at her, but she doesn't say anything. Instead she swallows hard, and then both of us are walking toward the bedroom doorway.

Something catches my eye to my left. There's a fire-place opposite the bed, and beside the hearth is a small rack with iron fireplace tools.

I grab the poker and grip it tightly, wielding it in front

of me like a sword as we move out of the bedroom and back out into the hallway.

The music is even louder out here. What is normally a light, bouncy song carries through the empty halls in such a way that it's taken on a haunting tone. All I can do is wonder what we're going to find downstairs.

Carol clutches my arm tightly as we inch closer to the gigantic stairwell. I peer over the balcony railing to the floor below, but there isn't much of a view beside the entryway and front door.

I don't see any wet footprints or anything like that. That does little to make the lump in my throat go down. All it means is whoever's down there was here all along.

As the song ends, the house fills with silence again. Carol and I stop moving.

Then a new song picks up—"Frosty the Snowman". Carol scoffs but still hasn't let go of my arm.

We reach the top of the staircase. I come up against the wall with my back, brandishing the poker out in front of me. Slowly, one at a time, we descend the stairs, the rest of the room coming into view as we get closer to the first floor.

My heart feels like it's beating a hundred times a minute, and the sweat in my palm makes the poker tough to grip. Licking my lips, I take another step down.

From my position on the staircase now, I can see practically the entirety of the living room.

There's no one near the bookshelf with the music control. No one by the mantle, either. Everything sits exactly as it did the last time I looked around, but I still don't lower the poker.

All of this is just too weird.

The longer we go without any surprises however, the more I can feel Carol's grip lessen on my forearm.

By the time we reach the bottom step, she's not even holding onto me.

Still, neither of us is in a real hurry to step away from the relative safety of the wall forming one side of the staircase. I stare out at the room around us, my body still tense. I don't know what's supposed to come next.

Music just doesn't start playing on its own... does it?

The more I think about it, the more I start to wonder. Maybe the sound setup is on some type of automatic play system, and the pause button I pushed only pauses it temporarily.

We must spend almost five minutes pinned to the wall before Carol suddenly pushes off the last step, striding hard across the floor toward the bookcase. She walks right up to the tablet and taps the screen.

Instantly the music shuts off, plunging the house into total silence once again. The last note hangs in the air as I hear myself swallow.

"Funny. If you're here Nick, I'm done," Carol shouts, doing a spin.

"If you don't come out right now, we're *never* getting back together. That's what you wanted me here for, isn't it?" she shouts.

"Last chance," she finishes, and then the house is quiet again.

We wait, the seconds stretching into a minute. Not so much as a bump or creak, save for the gusts of snow against the glass panes of the windows.

Carol throws up her hands. "I don't know. I guess it turned itself on. If Nick were here, he would've come out."

Slowly I peel myself off the wall, but I am still not entirely ready to drop the poker.

"But what's the point of us being here, if he isn't?" I ask, my throat dry.

"I don't know," Carol says, shaking her head.

"There has to be some explanation for all of this. Something we just aren't..."

The way her sentence trails off pulls my attention away from the windows and back to her. But she's not looking at me. She's looking at the gigantic Christmas tree.

"What?" I ask.

Carol doesn't respond, just takes a few unsteady steps closer to it.

"Carol, what is it?" I ask, my heart picking up again.

She stops abruptly, and I nearly careen right into her. Slowly her hand comes up to point, and I see that it's trembling.

"That present," she says, her voice barely above a whisper, "it's *bleeding*."

EIGHT

It takes me a moment to comprehend what she just said.

Then my eyes fall to where she's pointing, and I no longer need to. I see it too.

One of the shiny wrapped presents beneath the tree, its corner a dark red. There's more red fluid forming a tiny puddle where the corner of the package touches the floorboards.

Carol's right. It *is* bleeding.

Why is it bleeding?

It's a question too horrible to answer, and yet we need to know. As we draw closer, the pit in my stomach only continues to grow. I can hardly swallow, my throat is so tight.

The two of us advance slowly, eyes locked on the present.

I can feel the heat of the fireplace to our right against my skin, warming it though inside I feel a deep chill a roaring inferno couldn't thaw.

The shadows dance along the wall, jeering at us.

We stop in front of the gift box. I can't pull my eyes away from that bloody corner.

The box is pretty big, maybe two feet by two feet. The metallic green of the wrapping paper reflects the firelight as Carol squats down in front of it.

She's breathing heavily. I'm gripping the fire poker so tightly it feels like I might snap it in half.

Carol licks her lips and looks back at me. I say nothing. Slowly, she reaches forward and starts to undo the big red bow.

The ribbon comes loose and flops to the floor, leaving just the shiny wrapping paper.

Carol pulls at it, ripping it apart to reveal a plain cardboard box. Only a single piece of tape is holding the two top flaps together.

Swallowing, I nod for Carol to pull it off. She does, and the flaps come springing open.

Carol looks inside. Then she screams.

I jerk as she scrambles backwards from the present, her breathing coming in short gasps as she hyperventilates.

"What? What?" I ask, feeling tears prick at my eyes.

. Her sudden show of emotion is utterly terrifying—and yet I need to know what's inside.

Carol's face is pale as she crawls away. She says nothing, her wide eyes still staring at the box as she shakes her head.

I peer inside. Then I'm screaming, too.

Inside the present box is a severed arm. A human arm.

But that's not all. I recognize the tattoo on the forearm.

My ex-boyfriend's arm.

NINE

Nick's tattoo is unmistakable.

Black and grey trees and wolves on his forearm. That's how I know instantly, even in the firelight, that the arm in the box is Nick's.

Before I can produce another coherent thought, I find myself vomiting. It feels almost involuntary.

The coffee from this morning burns my throat as I empty my guts onto the hardwood floor.

Carol isn't faring any better behind me. Tears streak down her face as she weeps and stares blankly at the box.

I'm panting, still hunched over my vomit. My eyes sting.

I just saw a severed human limb, cut off at the shoulder and folded to fit inside the box. Mentally, I'm still trying to process what I've just seen. It's like my brain is having trouble computing the data.

Nick's arm is not attached to his body. It's in a box. Two weeks ago, I saw him with both arms. Now...

My gaze is pulled back to the rest of the presents

underneath the tree. There are eight in total, including the one we just opened. My heart thuds again, and my stomach rolls.

Carol looks over at me. The same question seems to be occurring to her, as well. The same horrifying thought as to what might be in the rest of the boxes.

Pushing back to her feet, she takes a few unsteady steps toward the tree again.

"Carol..." I say.

Reaching down, she reaches for one of the smaller gift boxes. Maybe one foot by one foot. Her hands shake as she places them on either side of the box. Sniffling, she lifts it off the ground and then shakes it.

There's a wet thump and a spray of red drops across the floorboards.

Carol drops the package instantly as I gag again.

"Oh my—" she says, then shrieks as she looks down and sees some of the blood on her hands.

There's nothing left in my stomach to bring back up, but still I heave, my innards pressing together. This can't be real. I feel dizzy.

The heat from the fire blazes, feeling hotter than ever against my sweaty skin.

"We need to... we need..." Carol starts.

I nod, forcing down another gag. "We need to call the police. Right now."

Both of us go for our phones. With a horrified gasp, I realize there still isn't any service, same as before.

Carol starts crying again, her chest rising and falling rapidly as she reaches hyperventilation.

"I just... Nick," she babbles, her hand pressed against

her forehead as she taps her phone screen repeatedly, failing to get a connection.

With an angry grunt, she shoves back into her pocket.

What are we going to do? The snow is still coming down outside, and now it's dark. Pitch black, in fact.

There's no way we can go for help on foot. But I can't be trapped inside this house all night with the gift-wrapped remains of my ex-boyfriend under the Christmas tree.

Even the thought makes the world spin again. I bend over, putting my hands on my knees to stabilize myself, and to try to get my brain to function normally.

Suddenly Carol sucks in a breath. I look up at her. She wipes at her face.

"The landline. I remember it ringing last time I was here. That'll work, even in a snowstorm."

She runs off toward the other side of the house without waiting for me to respond. I want to follow after her, but the world is literally tilting at an angle right now. I'm not sure I can walk.

I don't know what's going on.

I don't know who did that to Nick.

I don't know who brought us here.

There are too many questions, and absolutely zero answers.

Then, just when I think things can't get any worse, there's a *pop*, and the house plunges into darkness as the power goes out.

TEN

Carol shrieks at the noise from somewhere in the other room.

The main room isn't in total darkness like the rest of the house. I've got the roaring fire behind me to thank for that.

Unfortunately, the glow only carries to the staircase. It dimly illuminates the winding steps we came down, the ornate carving of the bannister creating swirling shadows against the wall behind it.

Beyond the staircase, where Carol went, is completely dark. A void.

The side of my face burns with heat as my wide eyes peer into the abyss.

"You okay?" I shout to her.

I don't move a muscle as I wait for Carol's response. If I thought this place was creepy with the lights on, it's even more awful in the dark.

Rising up in front of me is the massive Christmas

tree, perched like a giant totem, its unlit strings of light-bulbs glinting.

The wind howls outside the walls of the old house, whistling against the glass as flakes of snow scrape against it.

But what I don't hear is Carol's voice. Inside, the house is quiet.

Too quiet.

"Carol? You okay?" I shout again.

My skin begins to crawl. Why isn't she answering?

Did something happen to her? *Someone?*

There's no response from the darkness. It's like the emptiness of this place just swallowed her up.

I know I heard her scream when the lights went out—so what happened?

Rising back to my feet, I look around for the poker. There it is. I pick it up, purposefully not looking at the open present box just off to my right.

The iron is slick in my grip as I start inching forward. Maybe Carol is hurt, having slipped in the dark or something.

Maybe she just screamed because she was as freaked out by the sudden blackout as I am.

"Carol?" I shout again, my voice coming out strained.

This time, I do get a response. A loud bang—like a door slamming shut. The sudden clap makes me jerk, my entire body stiffening.

I definitely didn't hear a door open. We would've heard it in the silence. But I definitely heard it close.

Someone has just left the house. My pulse pounds.

I'm at the edge of the fire's light now, squinting to try

and make out anything in the next room. It's really, really dark in there. I can just make out chairs, and what looks to be more high bookshelves.

A library or study, maybe?

The entire room lies dormant. I keep waiting for my eyes to adjust to the darkness, but it remains just as shrouded as ever.

After another few seconds, I step inside the room and away from the relative safety of the glow.

Windows to my right let in the tiniest bit of light that allow me to inch forward without tripping over something. I can just make out the shape of my hand as I hold it up in front of my face.

I manage to get through the room without knocking into anything. The entire time, all I can hear is my pulse in my ears. Still no sign of Carol. It's like she just disappeared, too. The house feels as empty as when I first arrived.

The fabric of my jeans creates a rustling sound that leaves me on edge as I move into the next room.

In a sudden explosion of noise, I hear the howling wind clearly as the door is blown open.

My gaze jerks over to the left and a wall with massive windows and two doors made of glass. Beyond them is a stone patio.

Snow blows through the opening and creates a small rectangle on the floor before the door claps shut again.

The remaining airborne flakes flutter down to the tile. With all the windows in front of me, there's enough light to see clearly that there are no prints on the floor inside the door. No wet marks that would signify someone coming and going.

There is, however, a trail of footsteps outside, leading away from the house.

They move directly from the door and the patio before disappearing into the dark.

My brow furrows as I stare at them. The only explanation is that Carol left. Why would she do that?

She said she was going to find the landline and then walked through this room to the doors without another word, without answering my calls to her.

Then apparently, she went off into the night without any warning.

Why would she do that, unless...

A new thought makes my mouth go dry.

I think back to the presents in the room behind me. Someone did that to Nick.

Someone summoned me here—and it's pretty obvious it wasn't my ex-boyfriend.

But what about my ex-boyfriend's jealous ex-girlfriend?

ELEVEN

The realization strikes me like a ton of bricks.

Carol showed up just minutes after I arrived. Coming out of the snowstorm, apparently so surprised to see me.

She said Nick had texted her, but Nick is in pieces under the Christmas tree.

She lied to me.

I never even asked to see the messages, simply because I had no reason to suspect anything. Carol seemed just as confused as me.

Then again, she and Nick did meet at a Broadway show. Even though she works on set design, she's got an acting background, same as he did.

I lick my lips, trying not to let myself get too overwhelmed.

Could Carol really have done this? The more I think about it, the more certain I am. This whole time, I've been wondering if there was someone else in the house. Some monster hiding in the shadows.

Turns out the monster was right beside me.

She knows the house. She said it herself. I think back to our conversation earlier, when she wondered aloud if this could've been some sort of revenge against us for leaving Nick.

Was she just toying with me, like a cat pawing at a mouse?

That trick with the landline fooled me, too. I didn't think for a moment she'd just slip off into the darkness.

But that brings back the big question at hand. Why leave? If this is a revenge plot, as she seemed to be implying, why leave?

She's already dealt with Nick, but I'm still here.

Unless I'm *supposed* to still be alive. My head comes back up, my throat tightening.

What if she's just framed me for Nick's death?

The idea sends a chill down my spine that nestles itself into my very bones.

There's concrete proof I was here, thanks to the driver of the rideshare who could say he dropped me off outside the front doors.

There's nothing tying Carol to the house at all. No texts. No eyewitnesses, apart from me.

And if the police find me here with Nick's body, whose word are they more likely to believe?

Carol wants to frame me for the murder of our ex-boyfriend.

She's going to take *both* of us down.

Now it's my turn to hyperventilate. My thoughts spiral as I think about how many fingerprints I've left all throughout this house. Not to mention the unmissable contents of my stomach.

I can't leave now, not even if I could manage it in the dark in the middle of a snowstorm.

If I do, the police will automatically assume I was the one who killed Nick.

But if I tell the police about Carol, they'll see it as nothing more than me trying to make my boyfriend's ex the scapegoat for my crimes.

I feel sick again. Bending over, I drop my hands to my knees and gasp for air.

This can't be happening. Not like this.

The wind scratches against the glass in front of me, howling with laughter at my fate.

How am I ever going to explain all of this to the police? They're never going to believe me—I don't even believe myself.

The world spins again as my face pulses with heat.

Then I let out a little shriek as the world around me floods with light again. The power is back on.

All at once, lamps flick on, the chandelier above glows to life, and the music pours through the halls.

This time, it's "Holly Jolly Christmas" by Michael Buble.

The coincidence of my name being in the song isn't what sends me careening backwards, my whole world collapsing in on itself.

It's the sight of Carol—lying dead just steps away from me in the corner.

A string of Christmas lights is wrapped tightly around her throat, their bulbs glowing a bright red.

TWELVE

I stumble backwards, unable to tear my eyes away from the horrific sight.

Because of the power outage, the corners of the room were so dark I didn't even see her. Her body was completely obscured by shadow, but not anymore.

A sob rises up within me as I struggle to get oxygen into my lungs.

Carol is dead. She wasn't framing me at all.

The string of lights around her neck looks like it's dug in deep. Some of the bulbs are shattered, leaving lines of red trailing down her neck from where the jagged edges cut into her.

The lights that aren't broken glow a bright, cheery red. Whoever killed her plugged the cord into the socket beside her.

I want to cry. What kind of sick person would do this?

At this point, I truly have no idea who could've done

this. At first, we thought it was Nick, then I thought it was Carol.

Now both of them are dead. I'm the only one still alive.

My head whips back to the footprints leading out across the patio.

Goosebumps rise across my skin as I stare at the clear impressions of someone's steps out in the mounds of snow.

Someone was *here*.

Inside the house, with us. The entire time.

All that calling, asking if someone was home. Turns out, someone was.

But who?

I suck down a breath. At this point, I don't care anymore. None of this matters. It's too much.

I'm trapped in this place with the remains of two people now.

Who knows if whoever did this is planning to come back? Given how sick this whole thing is, I don't want to wait around to find out. I need to leave—right now.

If I don't, I don't think I'll live to see Christmas Day.

The sound system goes quiet as "Holly Jolly Christmas" ends. The silence stretches for a few seconds, and then the music starts up again.

It's "Holly Jolly Christmas" *again*.

My entire body shivers in terror.

The chorus to "Holly Jolly Christmas" echoes through the halls, mocking me. It's so happy and light. Playful.

Like there aren't dead people everywhere in this house of horrors. Wiping my forehead, I stumble back through the library toward the front of the house. I need to get my coat.

I need to get my coat and my gloves and my hat and then run. I don't know where—just run. It's my only chance.

I won't be a part of whatever cruel game this is any longer. The snow is still coming down, but I'll take my chances.

In here, there is nothing but death. Out there, maybe I have a chance.

With the house lights back on, I'm able to sprint through the rooms, spilling back out into the main hall. My shoes squeak against the floor, the sharp noise nearly smothered by the music that blasts from the hidden speakers.

The tree once again sparkles with life and light. I don't dare look beneath it, instead locking my gaze on the coatrack inside the door. Carol's coat still hangs next to mine.

Maybe if I wear both, I'll last a little longer out in the elements. It's my only hope.

I come up to the rack, chest heaving and mind racing. Even though I saw the footprints leading away from the house out into the night, I don't feel safe. Not for a second.

In fact, I haven't felt safe since the moment I stepped inside the kitchen earlier today. Time to get out.

Hurriedly I slip my arms into the jacket sleeves, missing the hole once because of how much my hands are trembling. It's pure adrenaline coursing through me now, fight or flight.

Since I don't know who I'm fighting and I already know they're capable of using deadly force, I just need to run.

I get my jacket on and then reach for Carol's coat. She's slightly taller than me, so the sleeves hang down further on my hands, coming up to my knuckles.

I dig into my jacket pockets for my mittens, stuffing my hands into them before pulling on my hat. I don't know if it'll be any good, but I pull Carol's hat over mine, too.

Already I'm starting to feel the body heat trapped within so many layers. In a few more seconds, though, I'm sure I'll be wishing for hot flashes.

With the final zipper secured, I step toward the front doors without a second glance around.

Wrapping a gloved hand around one of the handles, I pull hard to move the heavy wood. It comes open with a creak, revealing not just the white-out snowstorm outside, but someone standing on the doorstep.

When I realize who it is, I'm left speechless.

THIRTEEN

Nick stands there grinning, a fuzzy red-and-white santa hat sitting atop his head.

I blink, not believing my eyes. How can he be alive?

I saw the parts of his body, all stacked and wrapped under the tree. I saw his arm.

My eyes flick down—to *both* of his hands.

He raises them up to the sides, wiggling his fingers.

"Hi Holly. Merry Christmas," he says, before his smile disappears and he shoves me with both hands.

I go flying inward, landing hard on my back and sliding almost a foot before coming to a stop. Nick steps inside and closes the door behind him, letting out a shiver.

"Whew. Cold out there, huh?" he says.

My back pulses with pain from where I landed on it. Nick is much, much bigger than I am.

When I first met him, I found it attractive that we had almost a foot difference in our height. Now, that absolutely terrifies me.

Pushing up to an elbow, I fight to get back to my feet. Nick shrugs off his coat and calmly hangs it on the rack.

"Bet you didn't see this coming, did you?" he asks me.

He smirks. "I was trying so hard not to make a peep when you and Carol were checking to see if you were alone."

His eyes fall to me. "Forgot to check the bathroom closet," he says in a sing-song voice as he waggles a scolding finger back and forth.

I pull myself up to my feet, holding onto one of the staircase posts, still wincing from my impact against the ground.

Some of it is fake, though. Even through my terror and shock, some part of my brain is still functioning.

The part that wants to live.

That part of me realizes that I'm still fully dressed to go out. If I can get a few steps head start on Nick, I can race back through the library and use the patio door. I know it's unlocked.

My pounding heartbeat clogs my throat as my mind races.

"It was easier than I expected to get you out here," Nick muses in a self-satisfied tone.

"You're so eager to get your little chef business off the ground. To think *that's* part of the reason you broke up with me. It's almost pitiful," he says, sneering.

I don't respond, wanting to save every morsel of my energy for the life-or-death sprint I'm about to make. I just need to wait for him to turn. If he–

There—he looked back outside.

I take off, shoes digging into the floor as I race toward

the library door. My entire body is on fire, my thoughts screaming as I lunge forward with every step.

He's got to be just behind...

He's not following me. Why isn't he following me?

I glance back toward him just as I reach the library doorway—and then I'm sprawled out across the hardwood floor, my palms and knees screaming in pain.

I tripped, but on what?

My eyes flick down to my feet, and I let out a groan. There's a string of lights pulled tight across the bottom of the doorway, the bulbs sticking out at all angles.

I know that wasn't there before.

I would've tripped on it in the dark when the power was out. But Nick couldn't have put it there, because I heard the door slam behind him when he went outside.

But that would mean...

Carol appears in my field of vision as she looks down at me, watching me gasp for breath. She's still got the trail of red lights around her neck, the wound looking bloody.

Nick comes to a stop in the doorway, rapping his knuckles against it.

"Oh. Yeah. Her too," he says.

FOURTEEN

For the second time tonight, I can't believe my eyes.

Carol is still alive. Not just alive but working with Nick.

Together. The two of them are in on this together.

She's got something in her hands. A bundled string of lights.

Nick hauls me to my feet and yanks my arms behind my back, and Carol begins wrapping the plastic cord tightly around them.

I try to fight back, but the wind was completely knocked out of me when I fell. It feels like there's no air in my lungs at all.

They cinch the string cord so tight I can feel the edges of it biting into my skin. With all the layers I've got on, my heaving chest feels like it's melting from the trapped heat.

"Isn't Carol talented? I thought the arm totally looked real too," Nick says as he starts dragging me back into the main room.

"Aw, thanks babe," Carol says.

Of course. Carol does set design and props for Broadway shows—if anyone could put together a realistic severed limb, it's her.

I'm completely bound now, unable to do much more than struggle against my binds as Nick deposits me in one of the leather armchairs by the fireplace, my arms pinned behind my back.

The heat from the fire is overwhelming, scalding my skin as Nick roughly spins the chair so I'm facing the fire full blast.

"Why are you doing this to me?" I ask, panting.

Nick ignores me as he and Carol step over to the tree.

Carol reaches into the open present box and pulls out the arm. It flops, and a splatter of blood splashes to the floor. She waves it.

"The magic of special effects. Pigs blood," she says, feigning horror before smiling.

I wriggle in the seat again. The cords are tied so tightly, I'm beginning to lose circulation in my hands. Already they're starting to feel cold and numb.

"You know, after you broke up with me, I had a real hard look at myself," Nick says, coming to a stop beside the fireplace.

The mantle is draped in a cheerful garland, and he props an elbow on it like he's posing for a Christmas card photo.

"And after a lot of reflecting... I realized *you* were the problem, not me."

I can barely move my hands now. My veins pulse where the cord is pressed up against them.

"See, I'm a star. Or going to be. Everyone knows it. I've got that It-factor... that willingness to go above and beyond."

"But you... you were holding me back," he says. "I can't shine with you weighing me down, you know? Thinking about you just makes me so upset, and I can't have that interference. So it's better if you just... aren't."

I don't respond, even though what he's saying raises goosebumps again. It's so hot inside my double jackets now that I'm feeling lightheaded. The world around me seems slightly fuzzy.

Before long, I might actually pass out. Maybe that would be a mercy. I'm not sure I want to be awake for whatever's coming next.

I tug my arm against the cords, but they still don't budge.

Carol comes up to Nick, putting a hand on him.

"What you did, Holly—he can't focus on his craft anymore, and that's a crime against all of us. Don't you get what you're depriving the world of? Obviously, you never truly loved him like I do."

Nick nods in agreement. It's true, I didn't love him. We only dated for six months, but I don't confirm their remarks because I've just realized something.

My eyes drift back to the broken bulbs that were around Carol's neck. She faked the bloody cuts with special effect makeup, but it's spurred an idea.

If I can break one of the bulbs, the sharp edge of the glass could be enough to cut through the plastic-sheathed cord strands wrapped around my wrists.

With my hands tied behind me, they won't be able to

see what I'm doing. As carefully as I can, I close my fingers around one of the light bulbs. My fingertips are slick with sweat, making it hard to grip the bulb properly.

To break it, I'm going to have to squeeze it as hard as I can. I'll probably cut my fingers, but it's my only option.

And no doubt a much less violent one than they have planned for me.

After a half-second to mentally prepare myself, I press down on the small glass bulb with all the strength in my fingers.

There's pressure, and then it gives—just as a spike of pain flashes up my hand. As expected, the glass cut into my finger. I can feel the hot blood pour down my finger tip. It takes everything in me to remain stony-faced.

"Carol helped me realize I can't truly be great until all distractions are gone. Together, we're going to conquer the world," Nick says, leaning in to kiss his ex-and-now-current girlfriend.

The sloppy kiss is disgusting enough to momentarily distract me from my mission.

"You know," I say, licking my lips, "I remember when you first mentioned her me saying you two probably just weren't a good fit. I was wrong—you two are perfect for each other."

While I'm talking, I'm rubbing the jagged edges of the shattered bulb against the bit of plastic-sheathed wire beside it. My wrist is absolutely burning from the odd angle and the exertion, but I don't let up. I can feel it working, and it gives me strength.

Nick adjusts his Santa hat as he and Carol finally pull apart.

"Thanks for saying that, Holly. Glad I have your blessing. It's always awkward with exes, you know? Though I guess it won't be for too much longer."

Nick steps away from Carol, who crosses her arms with a smirk as she watches Nick come closer to me.

His nearness makes me stop cutting the strand, as I don't want there to be any chance of him catching on to what I'm doing. Nick comes right up to me and then squats down.

"See, all I want for Christmas is you... dead."

FIFTEEN

My blood runs cold as the words leave his mouth.

He says it with a smile, like he's so clever. Carol snickers behind him.

When he stands back up to walk back over to her, I resume my cutting with more urgency than ever before.

"You're crazy. Both of you are," I hiss.

"Crazy about each other, maybe," Carol coos, her eyes finding Nick's.

"Anyway, what do *you* know? They say you have to be a little crazy, a little different than everyone else to succeed in this world. Maybe that's why you've been such a flop," Carol says.

"I won't let you hold him back any more," she vows. "He needs a clear head if he's going to practice his craft well."

I keep sawing through the cord. There's a shift in the air, like this conversation is starting to draw to a close. Soon enough, I'll be out of time.

I need to work faster. Push through the pain.

"You know," I say through gritted teeth, "he isn't really that good of an actor. Believe me—he dragged me to more shows than I can count."

I don't want to antagonize them, but I need to keep them talking somehow. I can feel the wire starting to thin.

My entire forearm is on fire now, the muscles screaming for me to stop.

But I know if I do, I'm going to die. I manage to push through the pain and keep sawing.

Nick's cheeks fill with color at my remark, exactly as I knew they would. Carol places a comforting hand on his arm.

"She's only saying that because she wants to keep you small. Exactly my point, babe. People with a fear of success want to pull everyone down with them."

Nick sneers at me. "See how supportive she is? That's what true companionship is all about. You never were there for me, and now I know why."

The music changes in the background. Now, it's "The Christmas Song" by Nat King Cole. Nick looks up, toward the bookshelves.

Then a smile crosses his face.

"Right, that reminds me—your present."

I still, my eyes coming up to meet his. I don't like the way Carol is grinning behind him. She looks almost... excited.

Nick takes another step toward me, and I recoil instinctually. The cutting slows as my throat tightens.

He pauses, pursing his lips.

"What, you don't want your gift?" he taunts.

"Carol, get it, would you?" Nick says over his shoulder, not taking his eyes off me.

I don't like the way he's looking at me. There's a cruel glint in his eyes that has my skin crawling. I dart my eyes over to Carol, who has reached under the tree for another present. This one is long and thin.

She undoes the bow, seeming to really be enjoying the tension as she works. "The Christmas Song" continues to tinkle on in the background.

I need to keep sawing, but I can't tear my eyes away from Carol.

Ripping off the wrapping paper reveals another box. She gets it open and lets it drop away.

I'm left staring at... a metal pole. A pipe maybe? It's maybe a few inches taller than I am. I blink, confused and terrified at the same time.

"We've all heard about roasting *chestnuts* on an open fire," Nick starts, his eyes sliding to the raging flames in the massive fireplace, "but what about roasting Holly?"

SIXTEEN

They're going to burn me alive.

Nick and Carol want to tie me to that pole and spit-roast me over a flame.

My eyes dart back to the fireplace behind Nick as I remember thinking I could lie down inside it. How horribly right I was.

I see now the two supports on either side of the chimney, metal brackets that the pole will rest atop.

My body begins to wriggle involuntarily as I shake my head.

"No," I say, sweat pouring from every pore on my body, "Nick, don't do this."

Nick doesn't even acknowledge me, instead bopping his head to the last few notes of the song. He lifts up a finger and taps out the final note as it rings out.

"Isn't that such a great song? Who knew it contained such good ideas, too."

Carol lowers the section of pipe to the floor and

reaches for another pile of Christmas lights that were tucked into the bottom of the box.

"Nick please," I say.

He still hasn't acknowledged me. Instead, he turns to Carol and asks if she's ready.

I'm out of time. These maniacs are going to tie me to the pole and literally roast me.

I renew the cutting efforts with all that I have left within me.

Suddenly—I feel the string of lights binding my hands go limp as the cord is severed. I keep my hands in position behind me so it appears that the tension is still there.

Inside though, my heart is thudding hard against my ribs. I'm free.

Now I just need to time my escape.

Off to our left is the entryway to the dining room. Beyond that is the kitchen, and the door I used to enter the house.

I don't know what'll happen when I get outside—but then again, I'm the only one still dressed for the weather. If Nick and Carol want to chase after me, they'll have to at least find some warm clothes, which gives me a few minutes' head start.

It's now or ever. As Nick walks up to Carol to help her with the pole, I leap up from the chair in a flurry of movement and sprint toward the dining room.

My sudden jump catches both of them off-guard, but their stupor lasts a mere second before they both snap into action.

There's the dining room entry.

My brain is screaming. Shouts from behind. Mere milliseconds before they catch up.

I'm inside now, rounding the table as quickly as I can while reaching over to throw a chair down into the path behind me. There's a crash as Nick trips over it, letting out a shout.

Darting through the rest of the room, I knock down more chairs to obscure the way. Anything to buy time. Seconds is all I need.

I jump through the doorway to the kitchen and spin, yanking the sliding pocket door closed, nearly managing to pull it all the way shut with a grunt when Nick's hand appears at the edge of the wood.

He shouts for Carol to help him as he tries to force the kitchen door open and back into its wall pocket. I push with everything I have, screaming as I put all my strength into bringing the door shut.

It comes closed, eliciting a howl of pain from Nick as his fingers get smashed against the wood of the door frame.

The pocket door bounces slightly as he yanks his hand out, and then I bring it fully closed and grab one of the wood cutting boards from the stack, jamming it into the narrow opening where the door slides in and out of the wall.

It barely fits into the slot, and I lift a meat mallet from its hook on the wall and pound it in even more tightly until it's wedged deep between the wall and the door.

My chest heaves as I take a step back, my vision spotty. Both of them pound on the door, shaking the wood in its track but not managing to budge it.

Turning around, I run up to the back doors.

Putting my hand on the doorhandle, I turn it and press with all my weight—only the door doesn't swing open. It doesn't budge at all.

Panic spikes across my brain as I throw myself against the double doors again, but it's no use. Something is blocking them from opening.

I hear Nick's muffled laughter through the kitchen door.

"Nice try. Blocked that off when I went outside. There's nowhere to go, Holly. You're trapped."

I can hardly hear him over the rushing of the blood in my ears.

No. It can't be.

My hands come up to my head, my cut finger leaking blood all over my hair as my legs threaten to collapse.

All of that for nothing.

I'm stuck in the house with them. Nowhere else to run.

Their pounding against the sliding door, and each thump impales me with another spear of fear. That door isn't nearly as thick as the front or side exterior doors.

As an interior door, it's only a few inches thick. They're going to break through eventually, and then they'll have me.

I blink hard, fighting back tears, as I scramble to focus my scattered mind. I can't just die here. Not like this. Not at their hands.

Glancing around, my eyes move to the rack of kitchen knives up against the wall to my right. If I'm going down, I'm going down fighting.

Stumbling over to it, I draw two of the biggest, clutching one in each hand. The sound of the knife blades scraping against the rack stops the pounding from outside the room.

My shoulders rise and fall as I blink hard to clear my vision. My entire body is tensed, eyes locked on the door.

"She's got the knives," I hear Nick say.

For a moment my spirits soar—maybe they'll leave me alone. Thanks to cooking school, I'm pretty talented with a blade, and I don't think they want to be sliced up tonight.

Then Nick speaks again, and I realize how screwed I truly am.

"Go get the guns, would you? They're in the billiard hall."

SEVENTEEN

I brought knives to a gun fight.

It's impossible to swallow around the lump in my throat as I hear the floorboards creak, telling me Carol is off to find the weapons.

They can't push the wedged door open, but they can certainly blast through it. Knives will do me no good if they have guns.

There's a light rapping at the kitchen door that brings my head up.

"So... yeah. In a couple of minutes we're gonna blow through this door, and then I'm going to shoot you," Nick says pleasantly.

"Regret breaking up with me yet?" he asks, sounding like he's pressed his mouth up against the wood.

"My only regret is not doing it sooner," I say.

I won't give him the satisfaction of collapsing in a pile of tears. There will be no blubbering for my life, pleading with them to spare me.

I know who Nick is now. What a monster he truly is.

"A fighter 'till the end," he says, teasing me. "There's the Holly I knew. Too bad it won't do you any good."

I look down at the cut on my finger. It pulses, blood still seeping from the wound. I can't just let them blast the door apart and then shoot me, too. I can't give up.

Think. I just need to think. It's so hard, given everything that's gone on today, but I've got to try.

I'm running out of time for the very last time. After this, there's no more plans. No more escapes.

When they come in here with guns, that'll be it, once and for all.

Licking my lips, I dart my eyes around the room. I'm in the kitchen, the heart of any home—not exactly a well-stocked defensive stronghold.

Then I blink as realization dawns.

I'm in the *kitchen*.

My territory. The place in the world I feel most comfortable.

As a chef, this is my domain. I know everything there is to know about this place—and everything about food.

Now how can I use that knowledge to save my life tonight?

My head snaps up to the pantry across the room. My pulse spikes, this time not from fear, but from hope.

Just maybe...

I shoot across the room, dropping the knives with a clatter on the kitchen island in the center of the space.

"Giving up? Wow, didn't expect that, honestly. Carol will be pleased," Nick says through the door.

Ignoring him, I yank open the pantry door and am greeted with all sorts of non-perishables.

My gaze flicks across rows of metal cans in search of what I need.

There. Despite everything, a smile breaks out across my face as I reach down for the big bag of flour stacked under one of the shelves.

It's heavy, probably about twenty pounds. Heaving it upright takes a lot, a grunt slipping out of my mouth as I shuffle out of the pantry.

"What's going in there?" Nick asks, "Sounds like you're giving birth or something."

My face is soaked in sweat as I bring the heavy bag of flour back out into the main kitchen area to set it down on the edge of the island. Once it's there, I smear my hand across my forehead and pick up the knife again.

"Found them," Carol's voice carries through the wood as she enters the dining room again to join Nick.

"Took you long enough. Sorry about the wait, Holly," Nick says.

I don't have long to do what I need to do. Without wasting another second, I slash the knife across the bag and cut it open.

Flour pours out in a white waterfall. Throwing the knife aside, I lift up the bag again, forcing more flour out. The bag is rapidly losing weight, making it possible for me to shake it all around, depositing flour absolutely everywhere.

The floor, the cabinets, the countertops, the air. It's everywhere, making me cough as the particles enter my lungs.

Stumbling away, I start pulling open every drawer to find what I'm looking for.

Outside the room, Nick and Carol talk in low voices. Then there's a gunshot, and chips of wood fly off the door.

"Coming in," Nick shouts.

My heart leaps up into my throat. There's flour in the air, but my plan isn't finished. I need to—

Here. Matches. Perfect.

Grabbing hold of the box, I race across the room toward the massive metal refrigerator. It's as tall as I am, and that's why it'll work, because after I do what I'm about to do, I'm going to need somewhere to hide.

Another loud bang followed by a thud as Nick kicks at the door. The frame splinters, and I hear a click as Nick cocks back the hammer on his gun.

This is it. I cast one last look around the room, eyes wild and head pounding. Particles of flour hang in the air, coating every imaginable surface.

As a chef, the danger of a dust explosion is well known. In fact, most carbohydrates, like flour, are combustible.

Packed flour in general isn't much of a problem, as it's thick and solid, leaving little room for oxygen. But in a dust form, tiny flammable particles with plenty of surface area for oxygen between them feed the fire, giving you an explosive, rapid expansion of flame.

It's identical to an explosion inside an internal combustion engine—in other words, not something you want in your kitchen.

But right now, I'm not following proper kitchen safety. I'm trying to blow up my crazy ex-boyfriend.

So when a second and final kick sends the kitchen

door collapsing inward, I yank open the fridge and then light the match before tossing it toward the door.

"And what to my wondering—" is all Nick manages before the explosion drowns out his voice and everything else.

EIGHTEEN

My eyes run with tears as I drop out of the fridge, my lungs gasping for air.

I can't hear a thing—only the ringing in my ears from the blast.

It literally looks like a bomb went off in here. The walls are marked black from the explosion.

Everything is on fire, smoke billowing out the blown-out windows at the top of the walls around me. The service entrance doors have been blown open too, providing a view of the dark, snowy night beyond the house.

With another wracking cough, I stagger back to my feet with a hand over my mouth to try and stop myself from inhaling too much smoke.

My impromptu plan definitely worked—but maybe a little too well. My eyes lock on the flames that seem to flicker over every available flammable surface. Already they're climbing the walls and staring to lick at the ceiling.

I dart my head around in search of Nick and Carol as my hearing begins to return.

I spot both of them in the dining room, out cold after having been knocked backwards by the force of the detonation.

Nick's eyebrows are completely singed off, and his pants are on fire. More pockets of fire have popped up in here too—the corner of the rug, the tablecloth.

The intensity of the flames is growing rapidly.

A fire alarm shrieks in my ears as I regain my five senses again. I stare down at Nick, who is bleeding from the ears. My ex-boyfriend.

I watch for only another second before grabbing a fabric napkin off the charred dining table and slapping out the growing fire on his pant leg.

These two are monsters, but I'm not.

And that's why we broke up.

Judging by the rate of the blaze around me, this whole place is going to burn. I can't leave them here to die, even after what they've done.

So while the fire alarms scream, and the fire continues to spread, I drag Nick and Carol out into the snow through the kitchen doors.

Once it's done, I stand over them, panting. My face is slick with sweat, both from the exertion and the heat of the burn from inside.

Nick wanted a nice, big fire to try and burn me alive. Well, looks like he got it.

Guess you could say that's *my* Christmas present to *him*.

After getting them both out, I run back inside one

final time for the handgun I saw on the floor of the dining room.

The fire has spread to the main living area now—I can hear the enormous Christmas tree crackling.

All the while, "Here Comes Santa Claus" by Elvis blasts through the speakers, the song barely audible over the incessant wailing of the fire alarm.

The icy temperature outside actually feels refreshing compared to the intense heat behind me as I step back out. Nick and Carol remain slumped up against the wall as I look up at the sky.

It's finally stopped snowing.

Listening to the crackle of the flames and the distant chorus of the cheery song, I plop down on a snowbank and blow out a breath. What a night.

Something explodes from deep within the house, prompting me to turn around. Against the darkness of the December night around me, the house glows like a beacon.

I can't help but give a delirious chuckle as I turn back around.

This Christmas Eve may not be merry, but it certainly is bright.

NINETEEN

My heart thuds heavily in my chest.

I can't look away.

I need to know what Kris's family thinks of my cooking.

After another nerve-wracking second, I see smiles and nods all the way down the table, and relief floods my body. The ham was a success.

A big win, especially after the events of yesterday.

It didn't take long for the fire trucks to arrive, even despite the inches of snow on the roads.

Given how dark it was, the flaming house and resulting smoke was visible for miles once the snow stopped falling. The firetrucks came wailing down the path, their wheels wrapped in heavy-duty tire chains.

I had to explain everything at least a couple times, and then a couple times again when they dropped me off at the police station.

Luckily, the firefighters were able to recover a few things from the house that matched my version of events.

Nick's phony severed arm survived the blaze and was the most compelling piece of evidence.

So I guess you could say that in the end, it looks like the thing that really held him back was his own hand.

Nick and Carol will be spending this Christmas—and many more to come—behind bars, where they can't hurt anyone else.

That leads us to now, with me preparing a Christmas Day late-afternoon meal for Kris and her family. It's only her, her parents, and her older brother, but it's everything I could've asked for. I get to do what I love, and it's the best gift of all.

My first customers—and judging by the looks on their faces, happy ones at that.

Their home is nice—nothing like the mansion Nick grew up in, but nice. A nice family home. And these friends feel like family.

Glancing out the window shows a winter wonderland outside, the street lamps glowing to life as the sun begins to set and makes the fallen snow glisten.

Music drifts through the house, and wouldn't you know it—it's "Holly Jolly Christmas" once again.

This time though, I don't mind it. As much as Nick tried to ruin the holiday for me, I actually feel closer to Christmas than ever before.

I learned things about myself. I know now that I'll never give up, no matter the odds. I also know I can do anything I set my mind to.

I blew up a house with a bag of flour, after all.

Chef Holly isn't going anywhere, and that's my gift to myself this year. I'll never give up on my dream.

So Merry Christmas to all—except you, Nick—and to all a good night.

THANK you so much for reading *The Night Before*. I hope you enjoyed it. If you'd like to read my FREE psychological thriller novella, The Weekend Trip, sign up for my newsletter by heading to jackdanebooks.com. As a member of my mailing list, you'll be the first to know whenever I have a new book release and get behind the scenes information on my stories and my writing life.

If you had a great reading experience with this story, would you mind taking a minute to post a review on Amazon? A few words is all it takes, and it will truly make a difference in my career as an author.

Reviews are so important in helping other readers find great books that are worth their valuable time and attention.

Thanks so much for reading, and have a Merry Christmas! :)

Jack

ALSO BY JACK DANE

ABOUT THE AUTHOR

Jack Dane writes thrillers and psychological fiction that largely takes place in New York City, where he lives. When not writing, Jack enjoys going to jazz clubs, taking people-watching walks in the Park, and exploring the city by night, where he picks up ideas for his next book.

Get a FREE copy of his thriller novella *The Weekend Trip* by heading to jackdanebooks.com

You can connect with Jack on Facebook as well!

Printed in Dunstable, United Kingdom